NIGHT OF FLAMES

PREQUEL TO SPACE COLONY ONE

J.J. GREEN

BOOK LIST

The books of Space Colony One

Prequel: Night of Flames
Book1: The Concordia Deception
Book 2: The Fila Epiphany
Book 3: The Scythian Crisis
Book 4: Interstellar Mission
Book 5: Humanity's Fight
Book 6: Final Onslaught
Book 7: Restitution
Book 8: Redeemer
Book 9: Reprisal

1

NIGHT OF FLAMES

He was barefoot, and the strange, mossy turf of the new world was rubbery and cool against his skin. After the night lamps of the barn, the outside world was pitch black to his eyes save for the string of lights that led to the latrine. He strained to listen. He was sure he'd heard the thunk of something large hitting the ground out there, but now he couldn't hear anything other than the wind rustling the fronds of vegetation that surrounded the camp.

Back in the newly built barn, the rest of the colonists were sleeping soundly. More than two hundred men and women lay on rows of low cots, exhausted after a long day spent bringing down essential supplies from the ship. It wasn't surprising that no one else had heard the noise.

The sound was probably nothing, he told himself. Maybe just a dying plant toppled by the wind. None of the probes the scientists had sent from Earth and from the ship over the years had found signs of complex animal life, nor of plants capable of locomotion.

Holding up a lamp and peering ahead, he went on. The lamp's glow wasn't strong, and the moonless planet with its faint, unfamiliar constellations was a dark place at night, but he had an idea of the direction the sound had come from. His eyes adjusted to the darkness as he went. Dim gray shapes came into view—the boxes of supplies piled in heaps around the compound.

Another thunk. He stopped. This noise had come from farther away than the first, in the direction of the comm module they'd set up to talk to the ship. He ran a hand through his hair and glanced back at the barn, tall and wide behind him, blacker than sky. Should he tell someone? Dr. Crowley, perhaps? One of the Woken, the doctor always seemed to know what to do.

No. The old woman needed her rest, and he was just a Gen farmer. What did he know? Besides, what else would you expect on an alien planet but weird noises? He would walk the perimeter fence and satisfy himself there was no cause for alarm, then return to the barn and his well-earned slumber.

A third thunk. Off to his right. *What the...?* He swung around and gazed into the night. Beyond the dim circle of his lamp's light was nothing but darkness. He hesitated on the verge of returning and waking someone in authority, but he was sure he was nearly at the fence. It would only take him a moment to have a quick look around. He decided to go on.

A shriek splintered the calm of the night. The cry had come from the barn. *Lauren.* An almost inhuman howl of agony shot through with terror followed the shriek. He sprinted back the way he'd come, his bare feet struggling to grip the damp ground cover. He slipped and fell. The lamp sprang from his hand and skittered away.

He leapt up. The lamp could wait. The shriek had been joined by shouts and screams. The barn doors flew open and people poured out. *Lauren. Where was she?* The people raced off, spreading in disorder throughout the camp, pushing each other down in their hurry to get away. The fallen couldn't stand

and others tumbled over them, crushing them in the stampede.

He was at the barn. He forced his way against the tide of escaping colonists. A woman came rushing toward him, her eyes popping and her mouth wide. She held up bloody, raw hands, palms out.

"Don't touch it," she wailed. "It burns." Then she was gone.

Behind the remnants of the people rushing from the barn lay the object of their fear: A grayish-brown mass covered most of one of the cots, leaving only the cot legs visible beneath the misshapen lump.

A man ran past, colliding with Ethan's shoulder.

"We can't get it off of her," he said, his deep voice choked with barely suppressed sobs. "We've tried everything. I'm going to call the ship."

The barn was nearly empty now. Only the brown thing remained and a young woman standing over it, hitting it with the broken leg of a cot, her face wracked with anguish and despair.

"Lauren," he shouted.

"Ethan," she exclaimed. She threw down the cot leg, ran to him and grabbed his arms. "Where have you been? The others all panicked and ran away. Can you help? Only don't touch it, it—"

"It burns. I know. Someone told me."

Ethan stepped closer to the thing for a better look. As he saw what lay beneath it, the strength went from his legs and he nearly collapsed. Poking out from the upper end of the creature were the head and shoulders of Dr. Crowley. The alien life form was on top of her.

"We can't move it," said Lauren. "It's stuck to her like glue, and we can't even touch it because its skin is caustic."

Dr. Crowley was still alive, barely. The shriek Ethan had heard must have been hers. Whatever the creature was doing to her, it had nearly finished the job. The doctor's eyes were half-closed and her lips were blue. The organism was suffocating her or—Ethan recalled that its skin burned—was it digesting her?

He turned to try to find something to lever the thing off the woman. There had to be something no one else had tried. But the thought of what the creature was doing to Dr. Crowley overwhelmed him. Blood drained from his head and he became dizzy. He fell to his knees, vomit erupting from his stomach.

"What?" said Lauren.

Ethan looked up. She was bending over Dr. Crowley, trying to catch the doctor's words.

"Don't go near that thing," he exclaimed, forcing himself to his feet and drawing his arm across his bile-stained mouth.

"The what?" Lauren repeated. "The...the fence?" She turned puzzled eyes to Ethan.

The fence? The electric fence. How had the creature gotten into the camp? Why hadn't the fence stopped it? The thunk he'd heard must have been the organism hitting the ground. And he'd heard more of them. More of them were in the camp. Where were the rest of the creatures? And where were all the people who had run out of the barn?

"Lauren, we have to go," he said. "I think the fence might have shorted, and there are more of those things inside the compound with us."

Dr. Crowley was the only Woken Ethan had gotten to know.

She'd been one of the first to emerge healthy and sound from her hundred and eighty-four years spent in a twilight state somewhere between hibernation and death as the *Nova Fortuna* carried them to their new home. Just as the Manual instructed, the Gens had begun to revive the founders of the mission two years before Arrival. Of those they attempted to return to life, more than fifty percent didn't survive the process, and those they managed to wake suffered strokes and aneurysms, or had brain damage, or were blind, or their limbs turned gangrenous when blood flow could not be restored.

Dr. Crowley had been standing in Main Park beneath The Clock when Ethan first saw her on his morning run. She was looking at the glowing figures that counted down, not up. Figures that marked the seconds, hours, days, months, and years that passed on their deep space flight.

At the sight of Dr. Crowley gazing transfixed at The Clock, Ethan had been reminded of the time when he found out what it was measuring. He'd been in kindergarten, and the teacher had explained that the children were lucky Gens who would be alive when the *Nova Fortuna* reached her destination. Soon after they were grown up, the teacher had said, they would leave the ship and travel a short distance to a planet where they would live out the rest of their lives.

Dr. Crowley's fascination with The Clock had made sense to Ethan. The figures on its display had counted down nearly two centuries while she'd lain in her vat of frozen slush. Though he was usually a little intimidated by the enigmatic Woken with their odd dialects and distant eyes, he couldn't resist the temptation to talk to this one. She seemed more approachable than most of the others, who were aloof and stuck together.

He jogged over and stood next to her, joining her contemplation of the steadily counting figures of The Clock. The older woman seemed to sense his nervousness, for she smiled kindly at him.

"Do you have any plans for Arrival Day?" she asked.

"I guess I'll spend it with my girlfriend," Ethan replied. "Unless there's something ship-wide planned."

"I don't think so," Dr. Crowley said. "I believe the director intends for everyone to celebrate in their own way, as it will mean different things to different people. May I ask what your occupation is to be?"

Ethan shrugged. "Just a farmer. I didn't do too well at school." He gave an embarrassed smile.

Dr. Crowley frowned. "Forgive me for saying so, but you seem ashamed. Being a farmer's nothing to be ashamed of. Your job is just as important as anyone else's, Maybe *more* important than some. The colony won't last long without food."

When Ethan didn't react to her words, she tilted her head. "Don't you want to be a farmer?"

Ethan glanced around. No one seemed close enough to hear their conversation. He didn't like to express his discontent with his allotted role publicly. He wouldn't be punished as such, but failure to conform to the Mandate wouldn't do much for his reputation. "If I could have chosen, I would have been an explorer."

"Oh, now that's a fine profession," Dr. Crowley said. "Why didn't you select it? Surely you don't need good grades to be an explorer?"

"It's a Second Generation occupation." Ethan sighed. "Maybe if I have kids and they want to take over the farm when they're older I'll get my chance."

"No explorers?" Dr. Crowley exclaimed, loud enough to cause Ethan unease that they would be overheard.

"No explorers until the Second Gen," he said. "It's in the Manual."

"The Old Manual or the New Manual?" Dr. Crowley asked, narrowing her eyes. "As if I didn't know."

"The New, I think," Ethan replied, glad that he wasn't the object of the annoyance that began to cloud the doctor's features.

"Hmpf. I'll have a word with the director about that. Old Manual, New Manual..." She waggled a finger. "There's only one Manual, and that's the one I and the other founders wrote before we departed Earth. There was no talk then of drafting an *updated* version mid-voyage. What do you pups know of settling a planet? Living out your lives on a starship is hardly preparation for..." She paused and took a breath. Her gaze flicked to Ethan. "Forgive me. It's not your fault."

After she'd calmed down a little more, she gave a short laugh and said, "It's strange. You'd think that tens of light years would be sufficient distance to leave behind petty politics and meddling in the affairs of others. But wherever you go, there you are, I guess."

"Is...is that what you wanted?" Ethan asked. "To leave all that stuff behind on Earth?" He'd had no choice but to be born aboard the *Nova Fortuna* and become one of the first humans ever to set foot on an extrasolar planet. But the Woken had chosen to risk their lives for the opportunity. That had always struck him as odd. He imagined that Earth must have been a terrible place for them to want to leave it so badly, despite the positives that the vids and books showed.

"Yes, politics, and more," the doctor replied. "Much more, though I don't know if you can understand. Truth be told, I feared for what would happen to humankind. We seemed not to be progressing, but regressing. It wouldn't surprise me if the technology of the *Nova Fortuna* were the peak of human achievement and everything went downhill after we left. But it wasn't only that. My eyes were on the stars all my life. I was glad to come along, even though I knew I might never wake up."

"You think technology might not have progressed on Earth in all the time that's passed since we left?" Ethan asked.

"I'm almost certain of it," the doctor said.

"Why do you think that?"

"Mainly because in the years leading up to the departure of the *Nova Fortuna*, we seemed on the verge of inventing a Faster-Than-Light starship engine. Sure, the popular trend was against anything *unnatural,* and there were protests and demands that space travel funding be cut because it was *wrong* for humankind to leave its birthplace, but the scientists were close nonetheless. So close that some of the founders even wanted to postpone the *Nova Fortuna's* leaving date. Why spend two centuries traveling by fusion propulsion when you could arrive within a few years?

"Yet here we are, and there's no sign of anything from Earth. If an FTL engine had been invented while we were traveling, it would have caught up to us by now. We wouldn't be trying to decipher scrambled Earth comms sent decades ago. The fact that another ship hasn't followed us tells me a lot."

Ethan nodded. The Woken woman's way of explaining things made much more sense than many of his former teachers'. "So, what do you think Earth's like now?"

"So much time has passed...I really couldn't guess. Does it matter? We have a whole new future ahead for all two thousand, two hundred of us. The beginning of a new civilization." She returned her gaze to The Clock.

LAUREN HADN'T SEEMED to hear Ethan's words when he told her they had to check the fence. She was closing Dr. Crowley's eyes. "She's gone," she whispered.

Ethan heard her, but he couldn't process the words. He swallowed. "The fence," he repeated heavily. "We have to find the switch." He took Lauren's arm. "Come with me. Get away from that thing."

But Lauren was shaking her head. "I have to find Belle. I have to make sure she's okay." Belle was Lauren's nursery-mate. They'd been inseparable since they were three years old.

"There isn't time. She could be anywhere," Ethan said. "And

there are more of those creatures out there. I heard them dropping into the compound."

"No. I have to find her, Ethan. She'll be terrified. You go and check the fence. I'll meet you at the comm module. I'll be careful."

Ethan closed his eyes. There was no time for him to think. There was no time for anything. "Okay. Okay. But please, stay the hell away from those creatures."

As Lauren ran off, calling for her friend, Ethan forced his reluctant legs to move. He was terrified of what might happen to Lauren, but he had to stop any more of the life forms entering the camp. He grabbed another night lamp and left the barn.

Ethan sped away on the quickest route to the fence. It had been the first thing to be erected after Arrival. The builders had sunk metal posts and fixed high-tensile alloy fencing to them four meters high and a meter below ground, enclosing the compound. But Ethan hadn't been a part of the building crew. Where was the switch to turn on the electricity? He didn't recall seeing it.

Another shriek split his ears. The noise came from somewhere to the right. Someone else had been caught by one of the creatures. Sweat ran from Ethan's pores at the memory of what had happened to Dr. Crowley—at the thought of what was happening to another person. The shriek evened out to a long, howling wail of someone in terrible torment.

The horrible cry stopped abruptly. Had the creature moved onto its victim's face? Had someone put the person out of their misery? Ethan steered his thoughts away from the idea. He had one goal: turn on the fence.

From out of nowhere, a child ran into his side and rebounded from the impact. The kid rolled to a halt and sat up, crying. Ethan went over, crouched down to the boy and held his arms. "Are you okay?"

"Mommy! I want my mommy." The child was only six or seven years old. He must have been separated from his parents in the mad rush from the barn. What was he even doing on the planet surface? Ethan wondered. He hadn't noticed the child during the day's work.

The boy continued to sob into his fists. Around them, screams and shouts were filling the air. Ethan didn't know what to do. He had to go to the fence, but he didn't want to leave the kid alone with those creatures roaming the camp.

"Come with me," he said, straightening up and holding out his hand. "Come on, we'll find your mommy."

The kid didn't look up. He buried his face further into his hands and shook his entire body from side to side, signaling his refusal of Ethan's offer.

"Come on," Ethan urged. "It isn't safe for you to be out here by yourself. Come with me. We'll find your mommy, I promise."

The kid lifted his head long enough to shout, "No, leave me alone," before he thrust his face into his hands once more and fresh sobs rocked his little body.

Ethan didn't have time to waste. He reached down and grabbed the kid, intending to carry him over his shoulder while he continued his search for the switch. But the boy struggled and kicked as Ethan lifted him.

"Whoa, take it easy," Ethan protested, trying to get a firm grip on the wriggling child. A small, booted foot struck Ethan full in the stomach. He grunted in pain and dropped the boy, who landed on his feet and ran the second he hit the ground, quickly disappearing into the darkness.

Ethan ran after him, but he couldn't see where he'd gone. He stopped and called out, telling the kid that it wasn't safe and that he had to come back, but he heard no response. The child was nowhere to be seen. Ethan's heart weighed heavy. He returned to his quest to find the switch.

THE BOY'S attachment to one of his parents—to the extent of refusing a stranger's offer of help—struck Ethan forcefully. He couldn't guess how that kind of attachment felt. It didn't seem so long ago that he'd been the kid's age, but he'd had no mother or father.

Ethan's earliest memories were of playing with other kids at his nursery. The nursery workers had been kind. He even remembered a few of them hugging and kissing him, their eyes teary, when it was time for him to go to kindergarten. But he hadn't developed the bonds with them that families were supposed to have. None of the care givers had been like a mother or father to him, as far as he'd understood the role. The only person he'd had that kind of relationship with had been Dr. Crowley.

He learned about families at school, and how the Manual instructed that, as Arrival drew nearer, Gens were to be encouraged to reproduce naturally and revert to the nuclear family patterns of human societies on Earth. The transition had to happen. The technology for artificial reproduction was wearing out, and it would be decades before they would be able to manufacture replacement parts.

Like the other Gen his age and all the babies decanted throughout the flight of the *Nova Fortuna*, Ethan's conception had taken place in vitro. The DNA codes of Gen ova and sperm and stored, frozen donations from Earth were carefully selected and matched to ensure maximum diversity. With a Gen population of just two thousand, inbreeding had to be avoided as much as possible. Even more dangerous was uncontrolled reproduction during the *Nova Fortuna's* voyage. The ship's enclosed habitat could not sustain a population growth greater than ten percent, or roughly the number of preserved founders they were bringing with them.

The lost boy had to have been one of the first naturally conceived. The Manual stated that the move away from artificial reproduction and toward creating families should start seven years before Arrival. Gens of reproductive age had to begin to get used to the new way of living before encountering the other stresses of colonization. Dr. Crowley had told Ethan of another reason behind the Manual's directive: the founders' thinking had been that Gens' new lives would be so much harder than living aboard the *Nova Fortuna* that they might need something to live *for*.

Ethan and Lauren had talked about conceiving a child, but she'd shuddered while lying in his arms and said the idea of something growing inside her was weird. Maybe she would feel different later, she'd said.

A SHAPE APPROACHED, long and low and moving fast. One of the creatures. Ethan swerved and ran away from it. For something as large as a man laid out and at least twice as wide, the thing moved quickly. He looked over his shoulder, but the life form was veering in another direction. It seemed to have given up pursuit, presumably in favor of slower prey. Ethan's stomach dropped as he remembered the boy.

The thing had scooted along the ground, its method of locomotion obscured by its overhanging bulk. But Ethan had no time to puzzle out how the life form moved. He was at the fence. His gaze roved it. No switch was in sight. A scream from another captured victim spurred him not to catch his breath before setting off to find the switch. He went right as shouts of terror, panic and despair resounded through the night and people cried out the names of their loved ones.

Fence wire and posts sped past Ethan as he ran. The dark scuttling figure of a creature climbing the far side of the fence flashed into view. Its scaly belly outlined with hundreds of insectoid legs reflected the light from his lamp. Ethan stopped and pushed the lamp between the wires at the underside of the organism, but at the touch of the metal its legs wrapped around the fence wires and clung to them tightly. Ethan couldn't move the creature, and he didn't have time to try harder.

A thunk sounded somewhere behind him. Another one of the creatures had made it over the fence. Ethan took off.

A flicker of something yellow appeared on the edge of his vision. Ethan stuck his heels into the spongy ground and skidded to a halt. A plastic handle jutted out from a post beneath a yellow hazard sign. He'd found the switch, but something was moving on the wires above it. One of the organisms was crawling over the post. Ethan raised his lamp to shine on the scrabbling life form. He had only a second before it would fall. He darted in and grabbed the switch.

But before he pushed down, he hesitated. What if someone were touching the fence? Turning on the electricity could kill them. He looked up at the creature that was about to drop. He couldn't help it. He had to take the chance. He pushed down the lever. As the electricity hit, the creature jolted, its legs jerking. It became rigid, and a terrible reek like burning rotten flesh assaulted Ethan's senses.

He'd done it. The electrified fence would prevent any more creatures from coming into the camp. But why had it been turned off in the first place? He shook his head. It was odd, but he didn't have time to think about it. He had to find Lauren.

Holding out his lamp in front of him, Ethan set off to search the compound. He hoped that Dr. Crowley was the only fatality, though going by some of the cries he heard echoing through the night, he doubted it.

It wasn't long before he came across the creature he'd tried to push off the fence. It had made it over the top and was lying inside the camp, but its back end had been in contact with a wire when Ethan had turned the electricity on. The life form was stiff, its thick hide was dark and charred, and it gave off a stench that made Ethan's stomach churn.

Liquid had spread out from the organism in its death throes. A puddle lay beneath it that had scorched the ground cover down to the soil. Pressing his elbow over his nose and mouth, he peered closer. The creature didn't seem to have any eyes, mouth, or other sensory organs. He shivered and drew away. How had the probes missed these life forms?

From somewhere to his left came the sound of someone running. He lifted the lamp as the person came into view. It was the director, though Ethan barely recognized the man. His gray hair stuck out all over and his eyes were wild. He grabbed Ethan's arm, making the lamp swing crazily.

"They're dead," he exclaimed. "So many people killed by those things. What can we do? Where can we hide? Do you know where to hide?" His fingers dug stiffly into Ethan's forearm, and his gaze darted from side to side. Sweat beads clung to the man's face despite the cool of the night.

"What the hell do you mean, where can we hide?" Ethan retorted. "We've got to find the creatures and kill them."

"We can't." The director's voice was wobbly and high, as if verging on hysteria. "Nothing kills them. Nothing. We've tried everything we can think of. And the comm module's dead. We can't contact the ship. They have no idea what's happening down here. We haven't any hope of rescue."

His grip on Ethan's arm was painful. Ethan peeled the man's fingers from his muscle. "The comm module's dead?"

"Broken." The director's eyes seemed about to leave their sockets. "Someone sabotaged it. We have no comm. We're alone down here."

The fence, and now the comm module? A scream, piercing and tortured, made them both jump.

"We have to help, not hide," Ethan said between his teeth. He pushed the man out of the way and ran toward the scream.

How had their hopes of a new, wonderful life turned to darkness and slaughter?

ETHAN REMEMBERED the director as everyone had watched the counting down of the final two hours remaining on The Clock. After a long, arduously fought election—to be the director who presided over Arrival and the first settlement—the man had stood straight-backed and proud on the podium in Main Park. His hair had been perfectly groomed, then.

The countdown had been breath-taking. Main Park held all the Gens and the Woken, and though there was no formal request for their presence, all but essential maintenance staff had gathered there. Some had even slept in the park overnight with the black, starry fake sky over their heads and the figures of The Clock glowing green in the dark.

The Clock spanned a wide section of the dome. As early as five or six years before Arrival, couples and groups had begun to stand beneath it and discuss their plans of what they were going to do when the *Nova Fortuna* reached its destination. Those who weren't drawn to The Clock spent hours watching vids on the planet they were approaching. As the ship drew nearer, visuals showed continents and seas and water-vapor clouds that seemed to confirm that everything the scientists had said about the planet was true.

On the final day, the murmuring of the crowd in Main Park had grown louder as more and more Gens and Woken arrived and excited chatter about the impending long-anticipated event rose, drowning out the circulation fans that whirred at top speed to renew and cool the air.

Ethan could hardly believe it when the moment that he'd been taught to anticipate all his life arrived. The final hour of The Clock flicked to zero to match the year, month, and day. Only minutes and seconds remained. The noise of the crowd grew almost painful. Then, strangely enough, the volume subsided as The Clock marked the final minutes, and then the final seconds, until only the quietest of whispers sounded among the more than two thousand people gathered underneath it.

The last few moments of their long voyage disappeared. One hundred and eighty-four years of waiting was over. The work of tens of thousands of people, many of whom had never set foot on the *Nova Fortuna*, many of whom had lived and died aboard her, were finally paid off. An almost deathly hush fell over the park.

Five. Four. Three. Two. One.

The Clock was a row of zeros. The device that had faithfully kept time for nearly two centuries stopped, its work done. Not a person in the crowd stirred, as if no one could quite believe they had reached this point—that the *Nova Fortuna* was in geosynchronous orbit above the site that was soon to become their new home.

Brilliant lights exploded across the surface of the dome, accompanied by ear-splitting bangs and whistles. The Gens stared up in fear, but the Woken seemed to know what was going on. They shouted and cheered and clapped and stamped their feet. Whatever the cascading colors were, they seemed to be celebrating the safe arrival of the colonists, and soon the Gens joined the Woken in hollers and shouts and hugs and kisses.

Ethan had grabbed Lauren and lifted her up. He swirled her around as she laughed and screamed. They celebrated all night.

LAUREN. He had to find her.

They'd agreed to meet at the comm module. Using the distant lights that led to the latrine as his guide, Ethan raced towards the meeting point, ignoring the fading protests of the desperate director. As Ethan drew closer to the spot, dark, swarming figures of men and women took shape.

The crowd was surging in a blind panic. People were shouting and crying. No one seemed to know what to do or where to go. Ethan went from person to person, trying to find Lauren, but she didn't seem to be among them. In the chaos, he despaired that he would ever find her. Someone had to organize these people.

He cupped his hands around his mouth. "Everyone, get tools from the stores," he shouted. "We have to find and kill the creatures."

"We've tried," growled a man nearby, lifting a sledgehammer in one hand. "Nothing kills them. Nothing. They're all over the place, and we can't contact the ship. We're dead. All of us. It's only a matter of time."

"No. We can't give up," said Ethan. There had to be a way. "Come with me back to the barn," he said to the man. "Maybe the creature that was in there has gone. If it has, everyone can go inside. We can barricade the doors and wait until morning, when the supply shuttle from the ship is due."

"No way," the man replied. "I'm not going near any of those things. I'm staying right here."

"But you're no safer here," said Ethan. "One of them could attack any minute."

"I said, I'm not going anywhere." The man lifted his hammer again threateningly, and his eyes glinted in the light from Ethan's lamp. Like the director, the man seemed to be barely holding himself together.

Ethan clenched his jaw. It was no use. Their soft lives aboard the *Nova Fortuna* meant they were entirely unprepared to deal with the emergency. And why had no one thought to set a watch while the others slept? They'd behaved like fools.

"No," a voice wailed on the far side of the comm module. "Help him. Please. Somebody help him." The victim's terrible shrieking began, and the man Ethan had been talking to threw down his sledgehammer and, gripping his ears, ran off.

Then, above the shouts, cries and moaning of the crowd came a sound that made Ethan's heart leap. It was Lauren's voice, and she was calling his name. He headed toward the sound, pushing others aside as he went.

She was calling his name over and over. She seemed close by, though it was hard to navigate in the darkness and the confusion of voices.

"Lauren," he shouted. "Lauren!" There she was.

She'd found Belle, and the two were standing together with their arms entwined. As Lauren saw him, her face broke into a smile of relief and happiness. She started forward.

"No," a man shouted behind her as he backed up fast. He moved so quickly, Lauren didn't have time to get out of his way. He knocked her down, and Belle turned and screamed as Lauren's arm was torn from hers. The man scrambled away as the scaly belly of one of the creatures reared up. Ethan leapt forward, but he was too late. The creature fell on top of Lauren, flattening her to the ground. Its wriggling legs disappeared as it hunkered down. Belle's hands flew to her face and she stumbled backwards, screaming.

The creature covered Lauren almost entirely. Only one of her feet remained visible, kicking. The crowd fled from the scene, scattering like cockroaches exposed to light. Ethan grabbed the creature's hide, desperately trying to lift it up. Agony shot through his hands as the caustic liquid it exuded burned his skin. Belle was frozen in horror.

"Move out of the way," commanded a voice, but Ethan barely heard. He felt a kick, and as he turned, light seared his eyes. A woman was standing behind him holding something Ethan had only ever seen in vids. Through blurring tears he saw she held dead fronds of the vegetation that surrounded the camp in each hand, and the fronds were on fire. Blue and yellow crackling flames spitting sparks rose from them.

"Here." The woman held out a burning frond. "You do that side."

Ethan took the burning plant, though the pain from his hand as he held it made him gasp. The woman thrust her flaming brand into the creature's back. Ethan ran to the far side and did the same, pushing the fire deep into the tough hide. A great convulsion shook the animal. Its domed form flexed upward and became concave, exposing jerking legs and a writhing underside. Strings of a white substance hung from it.

The fire from the brands set light to the creature's back, and the flames burned golden as they grew higher. The animal squirmed and bucked as if trying to rid itself of the blaze. With a sound like peeling plastic, it pulled away from Lauren and dashed off, twitching and weaving as it went.

Lauren's body was still. Ethan turned his head. The world was swimming around him as he fought to erase the image from his mind. Despite the light from the flames, darkness encroached the edges of his vision.

"I'm so sorry," the woman said.

Ethan had forgotten she was there. She was watching him, flamelight flickering over her dark skin and black eyes. The burning frond she'd given him lay on the ground where he'd unknowingly dropped it.

"Will you help me kill the rest?" she asked.

"I...I..." Ethan swallowed. He couldn't speak.

"Please. I'm very sorry about what happened to your friend," the woman said, "but you have to help me. We have to kill these creatures before they attack again."

Ethan nodded numbly. She was right. If no one did

anything, more people would die. Lauren wouldn't want him to stand there and weep over her while others were in danger.

"Yes," he muttered. "I can help." Wincing, he pulled his shirt over his head and wrapped it around his right hand before retrieving the burning brand. With his left hand he picked up the lamp he'd also dropped and slid it over his forearm.

"Thank you," said the woman. "Follow me. We'll light some more torches and share them out. Do you know where the director is? Are you his assistant or something?"

"No, I'm just a farmer."

"Really? I thought you must be someone in charge."

"Why would you think that?" Ethan had never been in charge of anything in his life.

"You were the only one with a lamp."

The woman led him to a pile of dead fronds that had fallen from vegetation overhanging the fence. Ethan's brand had nearly burned down. They lit more and carried them around the compound. People were attracted by the flames and approached them, their ravaged faces lit with tentative hope.

They handed out the burning brands and went back to light more.

THE WOMAN WAS one of the Woken. Even if Ethan hadn't seen her before, he knew that.

Though they wore the same clothes as everyone else, it was easy to tell the Woken apart. Their height varied more than the Gens', and their skin tone ranged from a deep, dark brown through tan and yellow tones to pale, pinkish white. Ethan guessed that the controlled breeding of Gens had resulted in an evening out of height and skin tone differences that were usual on Earth. Male Gens were taller than females, but they differed by only a few centimeters from each other, and all Gens' skin was colored light to medium-dark olive.

Ethan might have seen the woman before among the other Woken as they went around in their exclusive groups aboard the ship. He wasn't sure. But his clear memory of her was from when he'd boarded the shuttle that had brought him down to the planet surface.

The incident had stuck in his mind because it was one of the few times that he'd seen Dr. Crowley angry. She'd always been kind and patient with him when he'd asked her endless questions about Earth, and she'd never patronized him over his ignorance. Neither had she subtly punished his curiosity in the way his teachers had. It had been a joy to him to finally find someone who would answer him seriously and not refer him to a vid or the Manual, both of which only repeated the tedious teachings of his classes.

He'd been taken aback when he'd seen the ire on Dr. Crowley's face as he joined her in the line to board the shuttle—Lauren and Belle had gone on ahead. The black-haired woman had been striding away from the doctor, so he'd only seen her from behind, but the stiffness of her back indicated that she was also raging.

"Is something wrong?" Ethan asked.

Dr. Crowley expelled a short huff of frustration. "You probably don't want to open that can of worms, Ethan. Some people..." she said, her gaze on the retreating woman's figure, "some people are just unable to let things go."

"Oh." Ethan would have liked to know more, but Dr. Crowley's stormy face prevented him from pushing her.

"I mean," she exclaimed, "it's been nearly two centuries. It's time to *move on*."

Ethan nodded sympathetically, though he still had no idea what the doctor was talking about. He didn't think he'd ever seen her in such a passion. He wondered if she had some bad history with the other Woken woman from before the *Nova Fortuna* had left Earth.

He must have been looking puzzled because Dr. Crowley eyed his expression before giving a short laugh. Her anger drained from her face. Passing a hand across her brow, she shook her head and sighed. "I'm sorry, Ethan. I shouldn't have let her wind me up so badly. I'm a foolish old woman sometimes. My friend has her reasons for thinking as she does. She can't help being paranoid. I just wish she could understand that we need to look to the future now. The Earth we knew is far away and long ago."

The line to board the shuttle had shuffled forward without them, and the person waiting behind told them to move up.

Ethan's skin prickled with excitement at the idea of going down to the surface. The Planet or the New Home was how everyone referred to it. The Manual stated that the world should not have a name until the first settlement was built. Then, the colonists would hold the Naming Ceremony where everyone could put their suggestions forward and vote on a final choice through several elimination rounds.

Though he had no name for it, Ethan's heart raced whenever he imagined what the planet was like. He could hardly imagine how it would feel to breathe a natural atmosphere, to look up into a sky or at a far horizon, and to walk on the ground rather than a starship's deck. The *Nova Fortuna's* circumference and spin created artificial gravity to match that of the new planet, but Ethan was sure that treading its surface would feel very different.

They stepped aboard the shuttle, and Ethan's excitement quickly drove thoughts of Dr. Crowley's disagreement with the black-haired woman from his mind.

TOGETHER, Ethan and the dark-haired Woken woman organized teams to search the compound for the creatures and kill them with fire. Gradually, the tide began to turn, and the colonists began to take control.

As a patch of lightening sky and dimming of the stars signaled the rise of the new sun, the settlers began to slow down their sweeps of the encampment. Some had already stopped entirely and given themselves up to grieving over those who had died.

Ethan and the Woken woman went to the barn. Ethan spread a blanket over Dr. Crowley's remains after they'd set alight and driven off the creature that was still feeding on her.

After covering up Dr. Crowley, Ethan sat on a cot. Something inside him broke, and he put his head in his hands and bawled like a baby. He could hardly believe he would never speak to the doctor again; that they would never have one of their long conversations about Earth, hope, and the meaning of life ever again; that he would never see the faraway look in her faded blue eyes when she talked of her past.

And in the depths of his grief, he couldn't even begin to think of Lauren.

He became conscious of a hand on his shoulder. The Woken woman was sitting beside him.

"I'm so sorry," she said, silent tears streaming down her face. "Meredith was a wonderful woman."

Ethan realized she was referring to the doctor. He'd never even known her first name.

"She was," he said. "She was a good friend too."

The woman nodded. "I wish our last conversation hadn't been an argument."

Ethan swallowed and wiped his face with the shirt still wrapped around his hand. His skin was still raw from touching the creature that had killed Lauren. "What was the argument about?"

The woman glanced at the door of the barn before replying, "Did Meredith ever tell you that powerful anti-science factions on Earth protested the *Nova Fortuna* expedition?"

"Dr. Crowley did say a lot of people had turned against things they'd decided weren't natural."

"That's right," said the woman. "That was one of the reasons we decided to leave without waiting for the development of a Faster-Than-Light starship engine. We thought that if we waited much longer, the public sentiment against the project would become so strong that investment would be pulled and the whole thing would be canceled."

"But you made it, right?" Ethan said, wondering why these historical facts were still important enough to argue about.

"Yes, we made it. We got away. But..." The woman paused. "Hey, I don't know your name."

"Ethan."

"I'm Cariad," the woman said. "You did some great things tonight, Ethan. When everything was in chaos and everyone else was panicking, you stayed in control. Without your help, more people would have died."

He was about to object to her assessment, but she held up a hand to silence him.

"Whatever you think, what I said is true. I think I can trust you. I'm going to tell you something that I want you to keep secret until, and if, it becomes necessary that more people should know." She got up and checked outside the barn before returning to the cot.

"Before we departed Earth, I and some of the other founders suspected that one or more members of the Natural Movement had infiltrated the project and were planning to come with us, either as Gens or in suspended animation. We insisted that a cache of weapons be secreted aboard to fight them if necessary."

Ethan's eyebrows rose. "Weapons? But the Mandate says—"

"I know what the Mandate says. *The new world is to be free of the scourge of human conflict.* But we argued that if we were inadvertently bringing along factions who opposed our plan, we had to be able to defend ourselves against them." Cariad sighed. For a moment the passing of the years she'd spent in a near-death state showed in her features.

"It's an old argument," she went on, "but I believe weapons are a necessary evil. Sadly, most of those who agreed with me didn't survive the Waking process. A few are still suspended. I was the only one around to argue that we should bring the weapons down to the planet surface. That was what I was talking to Meredith about while we were waiting to board the shuttle. I was hoping to persuade her at the last minute. The *Nova Fortuna's* systems are heavily protected against sabotage. We made sure of that. If someone from the Natural Movement had wanted to jeopardize the settlement, the first opportunity would have been tonight."

"The electricity to the fence had been turned off," Ethan said. "And the director said the comm module had been sabotaged."

"Exactly."

"But...that's crazy. Whoever did those things would have been committing suicide."

"You have no idea how fanatical that Natural Movement was," Cariad said. "Many of them didn't hesitate to die for their cause."

"But..." Ethan's mind was whirring. "Do you think they knew about the creatures?"

"It's possible. They'd had infiltrated most areas of government and the scientific community. Someone could have easily *lost* some data."

"They're coming back," screamed a voice outside. "They're climbing the fence. Get the fire. We need more fire."

Ethan and Cariad raced out of the barn. While they'd been

talking the sky had brightened, and the edge of the rising sun was cresting the waving fronds surrounding the camp. At the now-visible fence, a patch of dark shapes moved.

Ethan ran over to see what was happening. His heart froze. The creatures were climbing over the bodies of their fellows that still clung tenaciously to the electrified wires. Whether some had sacrificed themselves to create a safe path for the others was impossible to tell, but the bridge of corpses was effective. The creatures were swarming across, and beyond the fence, hundreds, perhaps thousands of their squat grayish-brown bodies swarmed among the vegetation.

Cariad caught up to him. The color drained from her stricken face as she turned to Ethan and said, "I don't think there's anything left to burn."

The pile of dead vegetation that had fallen inside the fence had been almost entirely used up when they'd fought off the creatures' first attack, and the materials they'd brought from the ship wouldn't burn—deliberately so. But without fire, how could they kill the creatures?

The first shriek came. All the horror of the previous night returned to Ethan. Unless they could find a way to fight off the wave of creatures, they were all going to die in agony.

Cariad said, "What can we do?"

Slowly, Ethan shook his head. He was out of ideas. The weapons Cariad had mentioned were kilometers above them aboard the *Nova Fortuna*. But then Ethan recalled his idea the previous night.

"If we get everyone inside the barn..." he said.

"...we might last out until the shuttle returns," Cariad finished. "You take that half of the compound." She gestured right.

Another shriek resounded among the increasing screams, shouts, and cries.

Ethan started to run. "Go to the barn," he yelled at the colonists.

Cariad went in the opposite direction.

As Ethan ran and called out to the settlers, a terrifying thought occurred to him. What if everyone went to the barn and the creatures got inside too? They would be trapped, served up to the voracious organisms like dinner on a plate. But it was the only thing they could do.

All around Ethan, men and women were heeding his instruction and streaming past him on their way to the barn, but shrieks still ripped the air. More people were dying. Everywhere he looked, the creatures' low forms were roving the ground, looking for easy victims. It was only his speed as he ran that saved him from being targeted. He just hoped he could keep up his fast pace until he'd swept his half of the compound and returned to the barn. He hoped Cariad could too.

The sun was above the vegetation now, but Ethan estimated they had an hour or longer until the shuttle was due from the ship. He wasn't sure they could hold out that long from the sustained attack, nor how they could reach the safety of the shuttle when it finally arrived.

He'd reached the far end of the compound. His throat ached from shouting, and his leg muscles trembled from the exertion of running all night and morning. Exhaustion was making him want to retch.

A few of the creatures were motionless, hunched over on the ground, no doubt digesting the settlers they'd caught. More of them were roaming around, covering the distance between Ethan and the barn. To get to safety, he would have to run the gauntlet.

He set off. Deprived of slower prey in the nearly empty compound, the organisms closest to Ethan ceased their aimless wandering and turned as he sped past. As they turned, others farther away followed their movement and converged on him. He dug deep into his depleted reserves and sped up.

He was running for his life.

The barn drew closer quickly, but not quickly enough. The creatures were nearly upon him. One reared up in front of him. Ethan kicked the middle of its scaly belly. As the thing toppled onto its back, its nearest fellows fell upon it, covering it with their bodies and sticky white digestive fluid.

A creature ran across Ethan's path. He leapt over it and landed heavily on the other side, almost overbalancing. Somehow, he stayed upright and continued running, though sharp stabs of pain pierced his ankle.

The barn was only fifty meters or so distant. He just had to make it that far.

He was approaching the side of the barn, and creatures were swarming toward him around it, which meant that no one else was available for them to chase. Which meant... A wave of horror washed over him. He rounded the side of the barn. The doors were closed.

He was alone outside with the creatures.

The organisms were drawing rapidly closer. Ethan spun around. A hum sounded above him, but he couldn't take his eyes off the creatures that were surrounding him. They'd killed Dr. Crowley and Lauren and they were going to kill him too. All his short life aboard the *Nova Fortuna*, all the learning and preparation he'd done had come to this: A lonely, grisly death.

A squat, grayish-brown form made a run at him. He kicked the creature, lifting its edge, spinning it over and onto its back, where others quickly claimed it. Ethan's shock and fear were turning to anger, then rage. He was determined to die fighting.

Another creature approached and reared up. Ethan kicked that one too. He wondered how long he would last. Dimly, he heard the hum grow louder, but he couldn't pay it any mind. He had maybe another few seconds of life.

A shadow fell on his back, cooling the warmth of the morning sunlight. He turned. A massive creature, around three meters tall, was rearing up. Ethan ran directly at it, his head down, and butted it square in the middle.

But as he turned again, another was already rearing, closer this time. He stepped backward and tripped over the one that he'd just butted, or rather another that had clamped down upon it. Before he could do anything to save himself, he was on the ground. He struggled to rise, but as he put weight on his injured ankle his leg bent beneath him and he fell again.

This was it.

Ethan looked up at a descending mass of scales. His heart seemed to seize up along with the rest of his muscles. He held his breath and closed his eyes, waiting for the inevitable agony.

But nothing happened. He opened his eyes. Where the creature had been was the sky and a faint trail of vapor. The air was filled with fizzing sounds and the smell of burning. A brilliant light flashed. He covered his eyes with his arm. Too late. He was blinded. A green afterglow was all he could see.

Ethan squeezed his eyes shut and futilely shook his head to clear his vision. A deep bass rumbling resounded and the ground vibrated. It was the shuttle. The shuttle had arrived. But it was early, and the people aboard it were shooting the creatures with weapons. That didn't make sense. Cariad had said that the weapons cache had been a secret hardly anyone knew about.

The fizzing noise was dying down. An acrid reek choked Ethan, and he coughed and retched. Slowly, his sight was beginning to return. Something dark approached. One of the creatures. He shuffled backward on all fours, his burned palms shooting out bolts of pain.

"Whoa, take it easy," came a man's voice. "I'm not going to hurt you."

Ethan stopped and blinked in the direction of the voice.

The dark shape hadn't been a rearing creature. It was a man. Someone had come out of the barn to help him.

But as Ethan squinted up at the figure that was becoming more defined in his sight, his confusion increased. The man was wearing clothes of a type he'd never seen before. They were nothing like the clothes the *Nova Fortuna* colonists wore.

Behind the man was another puzzle. Ethan saw what looked like a shuttle craft, but it was much smaller than the *Nova Fortuna's*. The craft was also sleek and streamlined for speed.

"Can you stand?" asked the man. "There's nothing to be afraid of. We're exterminating the rest of your little infestation."

Ethan nodded, surprise stilling his tongue. The man reached down and grabbed Ethan's forearm, carefully avoiding his burnt hand, and pulled him to his feet. When Ethan wobbled on his sore ankle, the man pulled his arm across his shoulder for support.

"Come with me," he said. "I'll fix you up. We have medical supplies on board the ship." He began leading Ethan toward the shuttle.

"What..." Ethan croaked. He swallowed and coughed. "What's going on?"

THE WOMAN WAS white-faced and shaking as they led her out to the center of the compound three days later, but Ethan didn't feel even a twinge of pity. She'd been a nursery worker, of all things. He hadn't known her, and he was glad of it. He couldn't imagine what it would feel like to be the friend of someone responsible for so many horrible deaths. He couldn't imagine knowing someone closely and never guessing that they had been brought up from birth to ensure the failure of humankind's first extrasolar colony.

The sun was high and the day was warm. A steady wind stirred the fronds of vegetation around the camp as it had on that first, terrible night.

As she was marched to the spot where she would die in front of those who had volunteered to bear witness, the woman stumbled. The guards flanking her pulled her up and forced her to walk on. Her sobs rose above the rush of the wind.

Ethan's rescuer sat next to him. He couldn't help but think of the man and his shipmates as people from the future. Arriving at the last minute in humanity's first FTL ship, it seemed to Ethan that they were almost superhuman. With their state-of-the-art technology and advanced knowledge, they were vastly superior to him, a lowly farmer.

He wished that Lauren and Dr. Crowley were alive to meet the newcomers. His head sank low. He didn't think he would ever forgive himself for not preventing the deaths of the two people who were most important to him.

"You don't feel sorry for her, do you?" the man asked, mistaking his glum look.

Ethan shook his head. "So many people died. I wish I'd done more."

The man placed a friendly hand on his shoulder. "You were a hero. You turned on the electricity to the fence, and along with your friend you fought off the first wave of the creatures. You bought some time, long enough for us to arrive."

The man had explained after the attack as he was tending Ethan's wounds that decades previously archaeologists on Earth had stumbled upon the Natural Movement's plot to sabotage the colony in ancient computer files, but that the FTL Drive hadn't been invented until recently.

"I wish we could have made it here sooner," he continued, "but there was nothing we could do until we had the technology to catch up to you. I'm sorry. We came as soon as we could."

The saboteur was at her execution spot. She'd stopped weeping and was looking around her as if in a daze. Ethan had heard that even the truth drugs of the Earth humans hadn't made her divulge the names of any co-conspirators. He hoped she really was the only one.

One of the guards raised his weapon. The woman stood still, awaiting her death.

Ethan looked away.

The wind blew.

❀ Created with Vellum